W9-BGK-756

CINDERELLA

Charles Perrault

CINDERELLA

or

The Little Glass Slipper

illustrated by

SHIRLEY HUGHES

HENRY Z. WALCK, INC.

NEW YORK

```
398.2     Perrault, Charles
   P          Cinderella, or The little glass
          slipper; illus. by Shirley Hughes.
          Walck, 1971
             48p.  illus.

             First pub. in Great Britain in 1970.
          Notes by Kathleen Lines: p.48.
          This edition is based on a trans-
          lation by Robert Samber.


          1. Fairy tales   2. Folklore - France
          I. Illus.          II. Title
```

This Main Entry catalog card may be reproduced without permission.

Cinderella

Once upon a time there lived a gentleman who married, as his second wife, a handsome widow. She was however an excessively proud and ill-natured woman, and her two daughters were just like her. The man, on his side, also had a daughter, younger than her step-sisters, and she, taking after her own mother, was gentle, sweet and charming.

The wedding festivities were barely over when the woman showed her true character. She began to ill-treat her step-daughter, whose beauty and goodness made her own daughters seem all the more unattractive. The poor child was given all the rough household tasks to do. And while her step-sisters were surrounded

with every comfort and luxury and lived a life of ease, the younger girl swept and dusted their rooms, washed the dishes, scrubbed the floor and steps and worked from morning till night. Her room was a wretched attic at the top of the house, and her bed a mattress filled with straw. She bore all this hardship with patience, not daring to complain to her father lest he should scold her, for he was quite under the thumb of his new wife.

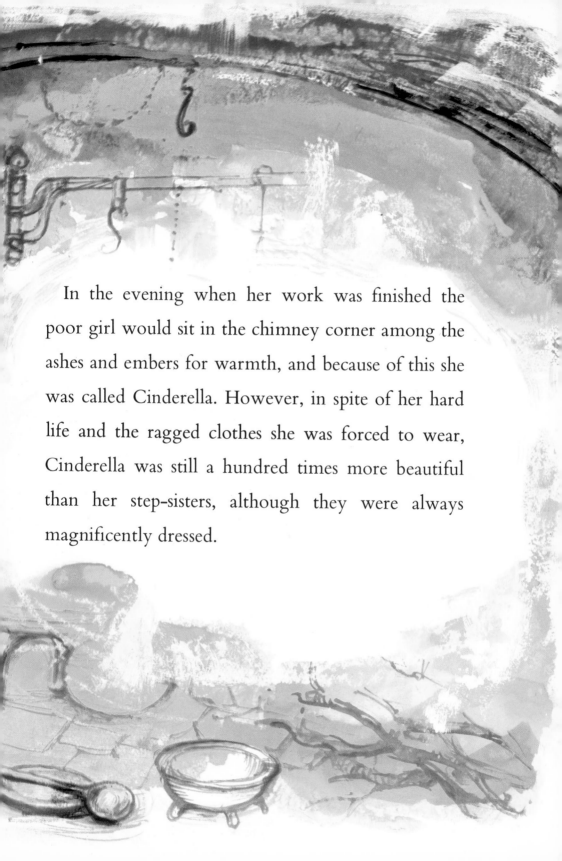

In the evening when her work was finished the poor girl would sit in the chimney corner among the ashes and embers for warmth, and because of this she was called Cinderella. However, in spite of her hard life and the ragged clothes she was forced to wear, Cinderella was still a hundred times more beautiful than her step-sisters, although they were always magnificently dressed.

Now it happened that the king's son was giving two balls, to which all persons of fashion were invited. Of course the two young ladies received an invitation, for they went out much into society. They were delighted, and for weeks did nothing but talk about what they

would wear. Cinderella was kept very busy washing and ironing and sewing for them. They ordered elaborate head-dresses from the best milliner, and the most expensive beauty preparations.

13

Cinderella was called upon to help and advise them, for she had excellent taste. She arranged their hair most expertly even though they cruelly teased her,

asking if she would not like to go to the balls, and saying how everyone would laugh to see a Cinder-wench among the fine ladies.

At last the happy moment for departure came, and off they all went. Cinderella followed them with her eyes for as long as she could, and when they were out of sight she sat down by the fireside and burst into tears. At that moment her fairy godmother appeared beside her. "What is the matter, dear child?" she said. "Why do you cry so bitterly?"

"I wish—oh, I wish . . ." Cinderella began, but tears choked her and she could not go on.

"You wish that you could go to the ball, is that it?" asked her godmother.

"Oh, yes I do," sobbed Cinderella.

"Well," said the old lady, "you are a good girl and I shall see to it. Go into the garden and fetch me a pumpkin." Cinderella did as she was bid and brought

the largest pumpkin she could find, but wondering all the while what use it could be. Her godmother scooped out the inside, leaving nothing but the rind, and then touched it with her wand. Instantly it became a splendid golden coach. After that she looked in the

mousetrap, and found there six live mice. She told Cinderella to lift up the trap door gently and as the mice ran out one by one, she tapped each one with her wand and it was turned into a horse. So here was a team of six dapple-grey carriage horses, only needing

a coachman. "I'll go and look at the rat-trap," said
Cinderella, "if there is a rat in it, we'll make a coachman
of him."

"You are right," said her godmother, "go and see."
There were three rats in the trap. The old lady chose
the one with the longest whiskers, and at the touch of
her wand, it became a fat jolly coachman with splendid
moustaches. Then she told Cinderella to fetch the six
lizards she would find behind the water-butt. These
were changed into six footmen, wearing smart livery,
who at once climbed up behind the coach as though
they had done nothing else all their lives.

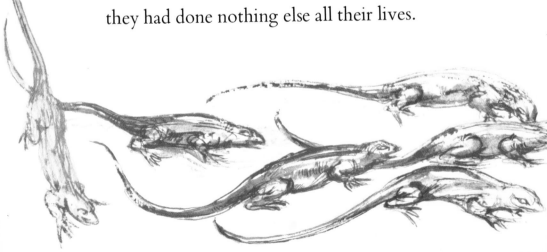

"There now," said her godmother, "you have your coach and all that is necessary to go to the ball. Are you pleased?"

"Oh, yes, dear godmother," answered Cinderella. "But must I go dressed as I am in these ugly, ragged clothes?"

Her godmother only just touched Cinderella with her wand, and in an instant her rags became a beautiful ball-gown made of cloth of gold and silver, and all sparkling with jewels. The old lady then gave her a pair of exquisite little glass slippers to put on. And now Cinderella got up into the coach ready to set out for the palace. But before she left her godmother solemnly warned her to be home before the clock struck twelve. At one minute after midnight her coach would become a pumpkin again, the horses mice, the footmen lizards and Cinderella would find herself in her old clothes

once more. Cinderella promised to obey her godmother, and joyfully drove off to the ball.

The prince, who had been told that an unknown princess had arrived, himself hurried out to receive her. He gave her his hand as she alighted from the coach

and led her into the great hall where all the guests were dancing. When Cinderella entered the ballroom there was a moment's complete silence. Talking ceased, the

dancers stood still, and the violinists stopped playing—then there was a growing murmur, "Oh, how beautiful she is, how beautiful she is." Even the old king gazed on her with delight and said softly to the queen that it was many years since he had seen such a lovely young creature. All the women carefully studied her appearance in every detail, with the intention of dressing in the same way themselves, if such materials and clever dressmakers could be found.

The prince led Cinderella to a place of honour, and later he danced with her. A splendid supper was served but the prince was so lost in admiration of her grace and beauty that he could eat nothing. Cinderella

went and sat with her sisters and was most gracious and pleasant, even sharing with them fruit that the prince had given her. This kindness astonished them for they did not recognise her. Then Cinderella heard the clock strike eleven-and-three-quarters so she got up, made a curtsey to the company and quickly left the palace.

She found her godmother waiting for her at home.
After thanking her for a happy evening she pleaded to
be allowed to go again to the ball next day, since the

prince had particularly asked her. While she was telling her godmother everything that had occurred, her sisters returned. The fairy vanished and Cinderella went to open the door. "You are very late," she said, yawning and rubbing her eyes, as if she had just that moment woken up; although in truth she had not for one moment during their absence thought of sleep.

"If you had been to the ball," said one of the sisters, "you would not have wished to leave any earlier. The

most beautiful princess in the world was there."

"Yes," said the other, "and she sat by us and was very attentive."

Cinderella feigned indifference, but asked the name of the princess.

"No one knows," they answered, "and the king's son would give the world to find out who she is."

At this Cinderella sighed, and said, "How I wish I could see the beautiful princess."

The next evening the two sisters went again to the ball. Cinderella was there too, and was dressed even more splendidly than before. The prince was constantly by her side, paying her compliments and speaking tender words to her. He danced with no one else all evening. Cinderella was so happy that the time passed all too quickly, and she forgot her godmother's warning. The clock began to strike. It could only be eleven

she thought. But it was twelve o'clock! Cinderella
jumped up and ran, swiftly as a deer. The prince followed her but did not catch her. In her flight Cinderella

dropped one of her little glass slippers, and this the prince picked up carefully and carried, while he hunted everywhere for her in vain. The guards were questioned, but none had seen the princess leave.

Cinderella arrived home quite out of breath, without coach or footmen, and in her old clothes. Nothing was left of her finery but a little glass slipper, fellow to the one she had dropped.

When her step-sisters returned, Cinderella asked if the strange princess had been at the ball.

"Yes," they answered, "but she left as soon as the clock struck midnight, and in such haste that she dropped one of her little glass slippers. The prince has it." Then they told her that the prince must be very

much in love with the owner of the slipper since he had looked at no one else the whole evening.

They spoke truly, for a few days later it was pro-
claimed to the sound of trumpets that the prince would
marry the one whose foot the glass slipper exactly
fitted. What excitement there was! The Court

Chamberlain visited princesses first, and then the
duchesses and after that the ladies of the court, but all
to no purpose. At last he came to Cinderella's step-

sisters. Each one tried and tried to force her foot into the little slipper, but in vain. It was far too small.

Cinderella, who was watching and who knew her own slipper, said lightly, "Let me see if it will fit."

The two sisters burst out laughing and began to jeer at her. But the Chamberlain, looking at her closely, saw that she was very pretty and he said he had orders that all girls should try on the slipper and it was only right that she should have her chance. So he made Cinderella sit down and hold out her foot, and the little slipper went on easily and fitted as perfectly as if it had been moulded to her foot in wax.

The step-sisters were astonished, but they were even
more astounded when Cinderella took the other slipper
from her pocket and put it on. At that moment her
fairy godmother appeared, and with a touch of her

wand changed Cinderella's rags into more magnificent clothes than any she had worn before.

Then the step-sisters knew that Cinderella was the beautiful princess they had seen at the ball. They fell on their knees before her to beg forgiveness for their harsh and unkind treatment. She raised them up, and, as she kissed them, said that she forgave them with all her heart, and hoped they would always love her.

Cinderella was conducted to the prince. Their wedding took place the very next day.

Then Cinderella, who was as good as she was beautiful, brought her sisters to the palace, and soon married them to two noblemen of the court.

CINDERELLA

Charles Perrault's *Histoires ou Contes du temps passé; avec des Moralités* was first published in Paris in 1697. It was obviously intended for children, for the frontispiece shows a old woman telling stories to three spell-bound children—two boys and a girl, in flickering fire- and candle-light. On the wall hangs the famous notice, '*Contes de ma Mère l'Oye*', which brought 'Mother Goose' into the English language.

Of the eight fairy tales 'Cinderella' at once became a favourite. Perrault, who invented little, but in retelling old, rough, country lore, invested the stories with a courtly elegance and impressed on them the permanent stamp of his period, did, in 'Cinderella', invent the immortal fairy godmother, the pumpkin coach and the little glass slippers. (It matters not at all to children that 'to fit like a glove', or, like 'wax moulded to her foot' could hardly apply to slippers made of glass: nor that the word is a probable misreading of 'vair'. The little glass slipper is firmly part of the story's magic.) And these items remain constant, even in the badly-told, rehashed versions which proliferated over the years—*and* are still produced. In English-speaking countries 'Cinderella' is often assumed to be 'one of our own stories', the French flavour lost and the name of Perrault forgotten.

On the other hand, every folk-culture seems to have its own 'Cinderella' story. In Grimm it is 'Ashputtle', or 'Ashenputtle'; and it is to this version that many variants are related, when they are not true parallels, rather than to Perrault. There are many European stories belonging to the 'Cinderella' classification, and one or two in Great Britain; there is a North American Indian Huron Cinderella, and an attractive little-known story from *The Arabian Nights' Entertainment* (stories collected in Egypt during the fourteenth and fifteenth centuries), in which a tiny be-jewelled anklet plays the part of the slipper.

Historically, and because it so vividly evokes the period, the first English edition of Perrault is a most interesting relic. Even in the literal translation of certain words and phrases, which does not really give the meaning intended by the author, there is a certain unexpected charm.

It is important that a child's first introduction to 'Cinderella' should be the story as Perrault wrote it, and in a version that gives some idea of his mannered style. In a picture-book edition, however, the text must be free of archaic words which would be meaningless to a child of today. So, I have modified here and there; cutting a little, rearranging sentences, and occasionally amplifying a bald or ambiguous statement, but I have taken care not to distort the author's intention, or to change the old-time French atmosphere. The main source for this edition is a facsimile of the translation by Robert Samber.

The lovely and romantic illustrations by Shirley Hughes will be recognised instantly as accurate pictures of life in the France of Perrault's own time. KATHLEEN LINES